For José —MB

For Kate —GP

VIKING

An imprint of Penguin Random House LLC, New York

First published in the United States of America by Viking,
an imprint of Penguin Random House LLC, 2019

Visit us online at penguinrandomhouse.com

LIBRARY OF CONGRESS CATALOGING-IN-PUBLICATION DATA IS AVAILABLE.
ISBN 9780593113851

Manufactured in China
Book design by Greg Pizzoli and Jim Hoover   Set in Clarion MT Pro

10   9   8   7   6   5   4   3   2   1

BLASTS OFF!

Mac Barnett & Greg Pizzoli

Viking

1.

BAD
JACK

The Lady is mad at Jack.

The Lady is mad at Rex.

"Jack," she says, "we have to blast you to space."

"You too, Rex."

3, 2, 1 . . .
BLASTOFF!

Jack waves bye to Earth.
When will Jack be back?

He will not be back.

The Lady gave them
gas for a one-way trip.

Jack and Rex
blast past the sun.

The Lady smiles and
lies down for a nap.

Well, I guess that's that.

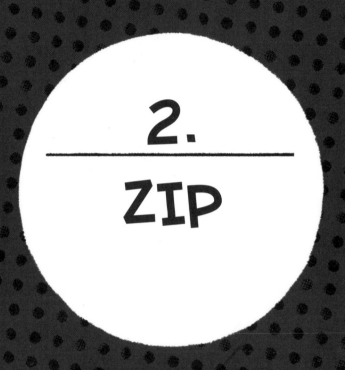

2.
___
ZIP

This is Zip.
Zip lands on
a far-off moon.

Zip has four arms.
Zip has three eyes.

Zip has a ship.

Hey, Zip! Nice ship!

Jack!

Oh, Jack.
This is bad.

This is a real mess.

Jack plants a flag.
That means this spot is his.

No fair, Jack.
Zip was here first.

Jack takes down
Zip's flag and
feeds it to Rex.

Jack! Give Zip
that flag back.
That's good, Jack.

Look, Jack and
Zip are friends!

Rex too!

3.

SPACE SNACKS

Zip fixes the ship.

Jack eats some snacks.

Jack, do you know
what would be nice?
It would be nice if you
shared your snacks!

Jack.

Share the snacks.

Jack!

Don't lick all the snacks!
Jack, that is very bad.

No one wants to eat
stuff that you licked.
Keep the snacks, Jack.

OK!
Zip fixes the ship.
Jack eats the snacks.
Rex eats a tool Zip really needs.

Look, Zip is bright red!
Oh, I think that is bad.

Zip says, "Creep peep."
That means "Go live over there."

Over there, where it is dark.

Bye, Jack.

You too, Rex.

4.

THE DARK SIDE OF THE MOON

This part of the
moon is dark.
It is dark and cold.

Oh, Jack.
Sad Jack.

Jack, at least you can plant your flag here!

Hey, Jack. The dark side
of the moon is not so bad.

Look, there is a big cave!
Look, there is a big rock!
Look, there is a big flag!

Say, Jack, what's on that flag?
It is some big thing.

The thing has a green eye.
The thing has big claws.
The thing has sharp teeth.
Rex, why do you bark?

It's the big thing from the flag!

Run, Jack, run!

Oh, Jack, run fast!
Fast, Jack! Go fast!
Back to the ship!

Look! There's Zip!
Zip and the ship!
Zip, let them in!

Zip blasts off.
Zip waves bye to Jack.

He waves again.
And again and again.

Here comes the big thing.

Oh, Jack.

Oh, Rex.

Look! Zip came back!
Yay! Zip saves Jack!
And Rex!

Now they can blast through space like three best friends!

Where will they go next?

5.

AND NOW: BACK ON EARTH

The Lady loves her
new life on Earth.

She makes art!
She makes cakes!

The art is great.
The cakes?
They're OK.

She paints and bakes
and takes big naps.

At night she sleeps.

What is that light?
Her house fills with light.

She wakes up,
it's so bright.

Three dark shapes
walk in the light.

It's Zip!
And Jack!
And Rex!

The Lady says, "Hi, Jack."

Zip says, "Beep deep."

That means "Take him back."

The Lady says, "No."
That means "I will
not take him back."

Zip says, "Zoom beep deep."

That means
"You must take him back."

Zip says,
"Zoom beep deep kaboom."

That means "Take him back
or I'll zap the whole Earth."

The Lady says, "Fine."

Jack, you are back!

Now, Jack: What did
you learn in space?

Bad Jack!

And Rex!

HOW TO DRAW...
ZIP!

IF YOU WANT MORE JACK, READ:

A JACK BOOK

HI, JACK!

Mac Barnett & Greg Pizzoli